THE
PRINCESS
AND THE
FROG

Movie Theater Storybook
& Movie Projector®

Adapted by Judy Katschke

Illustrated by Disney Storybook Artists

Reader's Digest
Children's Books®

Pleasantville, New York • Montréal, Québec • Bath, United Kingdom

The
Princess
and the
Frog

Not too long ago, in New
Orleans, there lived two girls
named Tiana and Charlotte.
One night, the friends listened as Tiana's

DISK I

I

mother read them a bedtime story, *The Frog Prince*. It was about a prince who was turned into a frog. Only a kiss from a princess could break the spell!

Charlotte would kiss a hundred frogs if it meant becoming a princess. But not Tiana! She dreamed of having her own restaurant someday. As soon as Tiana was old enough, she became a waitress at Duke's Diner.

Meanwhile, a handsome man named Prince Naveen had arrived in New Orleans for Mardi Gras, a big celebration. He and his valet, Lawrence, were going to attend a masquerade ball—at Charlotte's home. Charlotte would finally meet her prince!

Naveen danced down Bourbon Street with Lawrence stumbling behind. That's when a mysterious man stepped out of the

shadows. His name was Dr. Facilier and he promised to make their dreams come true. He held up a magic charm that looked like a small mask.

Then Facilier put the charm around Lawrence's neck. The voodoo spell made the valet transform into Prince Naveen. And it changed Prince Naveen too—into a frog!

At the ball, Tiana stood on a balcony in one of Charlotte's princess costumes and thought about her restaurant. After wishing hard, Tiana's eyes popped open. But all she saw was a frog. It was Naveen! Naveen urged Tiana to kiss him. If a princess kissed the frog he would turn back into a prince—just like in the story.

But after the kiss, Tiana turned into a frog too! Both frogs tumbled out the window and into the party below.

Tiana and Naveen grabbed onto a bunch of balloons that swept them up and toward the bayou. As they floated above the bayou, Tiana told Naveen that she wasn't a princess, but a waitress.

The balloons popped and Tiana and
Naveen fell into the water. The next day,
Tiana built a boat and the frogs met a
trumpet-playing alligator named Louis!
Louis thought that Mama Odie—the old
blind lady who lived in the deepest,
darkest part of the bayou—would know
how to break the spell.

As Tiana, Naveen, and Louis drifted

down the river, they became lost. Luckily, they met Ray, a Cajun firefly. Ray knew his way around the bayou and promised to take them to Mama Odie. As the four friends drifted toward Mama Odie's they talked about love. Tiana and Naveen shared a few secret glances—all this talk about love had them thinking about their feelings for each other.

But then suddenly—SNAP!—a giant
fishing net dropped over Naveen and
snatched him up! Tiana, Louis, and Ray
worked together to free their friend from
the frog hunters. Tiana and Naveen
hopped back and forth across the trappers'
boat. The frogs were too quick for the
hunters, and the men clubbed each other.

Everyone was getting hungry, so Tiana
decided to cook something for the group.
She gathered some mushrooms from the

riverbank and taught Naveen how to slice them into tiny pieces. Naveen was new to this—he'd never had to work at anything!

But as he chopped the mushrooms, he was proud to be able to help Tiana. And Tiana was happy to see how willing Naveen was to learn something new.

After a hearty dinner, the friends were full. Everyone was impressed by Tiana's cooking. "That was magnificent!" Naveen said. "You truly have a gift!"

While Louis played a tune on his
trumpet, Naveen and Tiana danced on a
lily pad. Tiana closed her eyes as Naveen
led her in the dance. Naveen leaned in for
a kiss, but Tiana reluctantly pulled back.
She knew how much Charlotte wanted to
marry Naveen and become a princess.
Tiana didn't want to think about her own
feelings for Naveen. Love was in the air...
but so was danger!

Dark shadows rose over the bayou and grabbed hold of Naveen. Tiana grabbed Naveen's arm, but her strength was no match for their evil. Even Louis wasn't strong enough to free Naveen from the determined shadows.

Things looked hopeless—until a blinding flash of light destroyed the shadows one by one! It was Mama Odie!

Mama Odie led the friends inside her
home. She told Naveen that he had until
midnight to kiss Charlotte, who would be
dressed as a princess for Mardi Gras. Once
Naveen had kissed a princess, he and
Tiana would become human again.

Midnight didn't give them much time so the friends jumped aboard a boat heading down the river. Meanwhile, Naveen had realized that he was in love with Tiana. But soon the shadows came back for Naveen and took him to Dr. Facilier. The power of the charm had worn off, and Lawrence was himself again.

Using the charm, Facilier turned Lawrence back into Prince Naveen. Then Facilier tossed the frog Naveen into a cage and locked it.

The riverboat docked but Tiana couldn't find Naveen. She knew just where to look for him—on Charlotte's float. Her friend would be dressed as a princess, all ready to give a kiss to a frog!

But when Tiana saw the float, she gasped. Standing on top of a wedding cake were Charlotte and Naveen, who was back to being a prince! But Tiana didn't know that she was seeing Lawrence. Sadly, she hopped away into a nearby cemetery.

Ray flew close to the float and freed Naveen from the cage. Naveen hopped out and onto Lawrence's back. Lawrence and Naveen fought over the charm. The frog tossed the charm into the air and Ray caught it. He headed to the cemetery.

Inside the cemetery, Ray quickly found Tiana and told her the truth about Naveen. Then he tossed the charm to Tiana and told her to run. Tiana hopped away as fast as she could. But she froze when she reached the gate. It was Facilier!

"Back off or I'll break this thing into a million pieces!" Tiana shouted as she held up the charm.

Facilier smiled and blew some powder into the air. A spell was cast, and Tiana was in her dream restaurant, as a human!

DISK 3

9

10

Facilier told Tiana that he would give her a restaurant in exchange for the charm. But Naveen would forever be a frog! Tiana hurled the charm to the ground, smashing it to tiny bits. She became a frog again. And Facilier's evil shadows swallowed him up!

Tiana hopped off to find Naveen and Charlotte. Tiana found them just as Naveen was promising to marry Charlotte and make her a princess, even though he and Tiana were in love. But there was one condition—Charlotte had to give Tiana

money for her restaurant. Tiana begged
Naveen not to marry Charlotte, and once
Charlotte saw that the two frogs were in
love, she kissed Naveen again and again
with no conditions. But because it was
after midnight, he was still a frog! "I'm so
sorry," Charlotte sighed.

Naveen wasn't. Neither was Tiana. They
were sad about still being frogs. But they
were in love.

The next morning in the bayou, Tiana
and Naveen happily exchanged wedding

vows. As their lips met—POOF—a flurry of magic dust swirled around and around the bride and groom.

When the magic dust cleared, Naveen and Tiana were no longer frogs. They were human again! As soon as Prince Naveen kissed Tiana, she became a princess. Her kiss broke the spell.

Soon a fancy restaurant serving food cooked by Princess Tiana stood in New Orleans. Tiana's lifelong dream had finally come true!

12